SCOOBY-DOO! PICTURE CLUE BOOK

THE CATNAPPED CAPER

by Maria S. Barbo

Illustrated by Duendes del Sur

Hello Reader - Level 1

ISBN 0-439-16010-3

28 27 26 25 24 23 22   40   10 11 12/0

Cover designed by Madalina Stefan and Mary Hall

Interiors designed by Mary Hall

Printed in the U.S.A.

First Scholastic printing, January 2000

SCHOLASTIC INC.

New York Toronto London Auckland Sydney
Mexico City New Delhi Hong Kong

and his friends were in

a .

Mrs. Blake's was missing!

There were strange noises in

the .

Could there be a ?

Let's look for clues, gang,"

said .

tripped and fell.

"Jinkies!" she cried. "I lost

my !"

 was looking on the

for her .

Did a take Velma's ?

was scared, but he knew

he had to help.

He went to search the .

4

 looked in the kitchen of

the  .

 was in the kitchen making

a  .

"Like, no  in here  ,"

 said.

 searched Shaggy's  .

But he did not find Velma's

 .

went up the .

He looked under a .

He looked behind a .

He found a .

But he did not find Velma's

 .

opened a .

He was in a bedroom of

the .

 looked under the .

"Rikes!" he yelled.

 found a under the .

But he did not find Velma's .

ran out through the .

He bumped into .

 found some clues.

"A is missing from the bedroom," he said.

Then saw a piece of thread from the on the .

went up the to the attic.

He slowly opened the .

 was scared.

There were a lot of

in the attic.

 found some .

But he did not find Velma's .

ran down the .

He found in the dining

room.

 and searched the table.

But they did not find Velma's

 .

 and looked out the .

"Like, I think I see something, 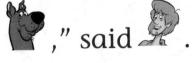 ," said .

They found in the garage.

"Looks like a is missing

here," said.

"And so are Velma's and

Mrs. Blake's !" said.

 and went back into

the .

They heard a noise coming

from behind the closet  .

and were afraid.

"Would you open the for

a  ?" asked.

shook his head.

"How about two ?" asked.

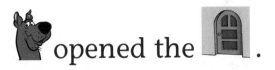 opened the 🚪.

The 🐱 and her 🐈 were

sleeping on the 🗺.

🐶 and his friends did not find

a 👻 in the 🏚.

The 🐱 had 🐈 !

And the 🐈 were playing with

Velma's 👓 .

"Scooby-Dooby Doo!"

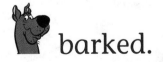 barked.

Did you spot all the picture clues in this Scooby-Doo mystery?

Each picture clue is on a flash card. Ask a grown-up to cut out the flash cards. Then try reading the words on the back of the cards. The pictures will be your clue.

Reading is fun with Scooby-Doo!

house	Scooby-Doo
ghost	cat
glasses	Velma

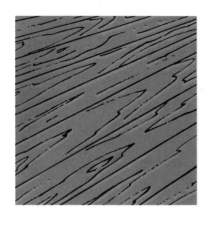

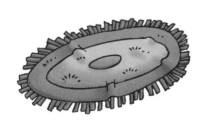

Shaggy	floor
stairs	sandwich
chair	rug

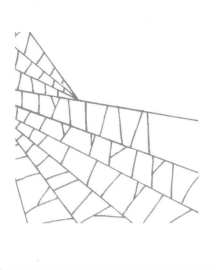

door	web
spider	bed
sheet	Fred

window	bats
box	Daphne
kittens	Scooby Snacks